Chapter 1
Pinky and Rex Get Dressed

"Wake up, Pinky!"

Pinky's eyes popped open. His little sister, Amanda, was jumping up and down on his bed. "Wake up, wake up!" she cried.

"I am awake," said Pinky. "Stop jumping on my bed!"

1

"We're going to the museum!"
Amanda shouted. She did not stop
jumping. "We're going to see the
dinosaurs! Hurry up, Pinky, get
dressed."

PINKY and REX

OTHER ALADDIN PAPERBACKS BY JAMES HOWE

PINKY and REX

by James Howe
illustrated by Melissa Sweet

READY-TO-READ

ALADDIN PAPERBACKS

First Aladdin Paperbacks edition September 1998

Text copyright © 1990 by James Howe
Illustrations copyright © 1990 by Melissa Sweet

Aladdin Paperbacks
An imprint of Simon & Schuster Children's Division
1230 Avenue of the Americas
New York, NY 10020

Also available in an Atheneum Books for Young Readers edition.

Manufactured in the United States of America
12 14 16 18 20 19 17 15 13

The Library of Congress has cataloged the hardcover edition as follows:
Howe, James.
Pinky and Rex / by James Howe ; illustrated by Melissa Sweet. —1st ed.
p.   cm.
Summary: Rex and her best friend, Pinky, each the proud possessor of twenty-seven stuffed
animals or dinosaurs, find their visit to the museum and its gift shop complicated by
Pinky's little sister, Amanda.
ISBN-13: 978-0-689-31454-4 ISBN-10: 0-689-31454-X (hc.)
[1. Museums—Fiction. 2. Friendship—Fiction. 3. Brothers and sisters—Fiction. 4. Toys—Fiction.]
I. Sweet, Melissa, ill.
PZ.H83727Pi   1990   [E]—dc19
89-30786
CIP   AC
ISBN-13: 978-0-689-82348-0 ISBN-10: 0-689-82348-7 (pbk.)

To my niece, Deborah

—J. H.

To Sandy and Max

—M. S.

Contents

Pinky got out of bed and ran to
the window. "Rex!" he called out.
"Rex!" he called again.

"Hi, Pinky!" Rex called back
from a window in the house across
the street. "I can't decide what to
wear to the museum today. Should I

3

wear my tyrannosaurus T-shirt or my
stegosaurus sweatshirt?"

"Wear your tyrannosaurus T-shirt,"
Pinky shouted. "It's too hot for a
sweatshirt. What do you think *I*
should wear—my shirt with pink and
white stripes or my shirt with pink
and blue checks?"

"I like the shirt with pink and blue
checks," said Rex. "It's my favorite."

"Mine, too," Pinky said. He had never thought that the shirt with pink and blue checks was his favorite. But now that he knew it was Rex's favorite, it was his, too.

"See you later," Pinky shouted.

"See you later," shouted Rex.

"What should *I* wear to the museum today?" Amanda asked her brother.

"Who cares?" said Pinky. And he went to brush his teeth.

Chapter 2
Too Many Animals

When he came back, Amanda was counting his stuffed animals.

"You have *too* many of these things," she said. "You should give me some."

"You say that every morning," said Pinky. "Besides, they're not things, they're my animals."

"But you *should*," Amanda insisted. "I have only thirteen animals and you have twenty-seven!"

"When did you learn to count that high?" Pinky asked, because he knew that she was right. He did have twenty-seven animals. And every morning, after he had gotten dressed and after Amanda had told him he had *too* many animals, he said goodbye to them. Each and every one.

He said goodbye to his frog. He said goodbye to his bear. He said goodbye to his kangaroo.

He said goodbye to his elephant, his giraffe, his three cats, his four dogs, his five rabbits, his alligator, his lion, and his tiger.

He said goodbye to his monkey.

He said goodbye to his mouse and
his moose and his mole.

Some animals he hugged
because they were little and needed
to be hugged. Some he patted
because they didn't care to be
hugged first thing in the morning.
And some, like his spider and his

porcupine, he didn't touch at all because they didn't care to be hugged ever.

He always saved his pig for last. Pretzel, named for his curly tail, was special. He had been given to Pinky when he was a baby, and Pinky loved him best.

In her room in the house across the street, Rex said goodbye to her friends, too. She had some bears and cats and even a pig, but she didn't love them best. Her special friends were her dinosaurs. She knew all their names and how to spell them (even the pterodactyl). In fact, Rex knew just about everything you might think there is to know about dinosaurs. And she loved them all. Each and every one.

After she had eaten her breakfast, Rex ran outside and across the street to Pinky's house.

"Pinky has twenty-seven animals," Amanda told her when she came to the door. "I counted."

"Really?" Rex said. "I have twenty-seven dinosaurs."

"That's too many," Amanda said. "You should give me some."

"Let's go!" Pinky's father
shouted, and everyone ran to the car.

Amanda climbed into the front
seat next to her father. Pinky and Rex
got into the backseat. "Does she
have to go with us?" Rex whispered.
Pinky gave her a look, as if to say,
"What can I do?"

Sometimes Pinky wished he was an only child like Rex. It was not easy having Amanda tag along on their friendship. He closed his eyes and hoped that Amanda would be gone when he opened them.

But then he felt Rex's fingers tickling him. He tickled her back. Soon he forgot all about Amanda,

who was busy in the front seat
counting the number of bug spots
on the windshield.

"I'm glad I have twenty-seven
dinosaurs and you have twenty-seven
animals," Rex told Pinky when they
stopped their tickling. "That way we
have everything the same!"

Pinky nodded his head. "We
have to have everything the same,"
he said. "We're best friends."

Chapter 3
At the Museum

The museum was a very big place full of interesting things to see. Pinky and Rex had been there many times. They knew just where the dinosaur room was, and they always saved it until the end.

"How much time do we have?" Pinky asked his father.

"We have about two hours," his
father said. "Then we'll go home for
lunch. Where shall we begin?"
"Dinosaurs!" Amanda cried.
Pinky and Rex looked at each other.
Amanda didn't know how to save the
best until last.

Pinky's father understood how Pinky and Rex felt about the dinosaur room. "Why don't we see something else first?" he said. "There's a new American Indian display. I read about it in the newspaper. Amanda, I'll bet you have never seen such a long canoe."

"I have never seen a canoe at all," said Amanda. "I don't even know what a canoe is. I want to see the dinosaurs."

"I know you do," said her father. "But first, let's take a look at this canoe."

"Good idea," said Pinky.

"Great idea," said Rex.

Amanda didn't say anything. She just scrunched up her face and crossed her arms.

Pinky and Rex agreed with
Pinky's father that the canoe was the

longest they had ever seen. Amanda
said it was just a boat and who cares?

Next, they saw the wild animals of North America and decided the bobcat was their favorite. Amanda said, "Who cares? They're all dead, anyway."

After that, they went to look at the minerals and ores. Rex thought the emeralds were prettiest. Pinky liked the quartz crystals. Amanda said, "They're only rocks. Who cares?"

Finally, after stopping every few minutes so Amanda could go to the bathroom or get a drink of water or pick something off the bottom of her shoe, they came to the dinosaur room.

"At last!" Rex said. "Now maybe she'll stop being such a grump!"

"Look, Amanda," said Pinky.
"Here are the dinosaurs."

"I'm hungry," said Amanda. "I
want to go home."

Pinky and Rex looked up at
Pinky's father. "Why don't Amanda
and I rest on this bench while you
look at the dinosaurs?" he said.
"Then we'll stop at the gift shop and
go home."

Rex grabbed Pinky's hand and
off they went. The last thing they
heard was Amanda saying, "Who
cares about a bunch of bones?"

Chapter 4
Amanda to the Rescue

Rex loved the gift shop. There were so many dinosaur things to buy. The problem was that she had them all. She had every dinosaur T-shirt, and every dinosaur glass, and every dinosaur pencil and pin and poster.

Pinky loved the gift shop, too. He always liked to see what new

animals they had. This time, he saw
that there were some new bears and
tigers and elephants. But he already
had a bear and a tiger and an elephant.
Besides, they cost more money
than he had to spend. And they
didn't have a speck of pink on them
anywhere.

Amanda stood in the middle of the store, with her arms crossed. "I want something," she said. "But I don't know *what!*"

All at once, Pinky looked up and
saw just what it was he wanted. It was
pink, and it was a kind of animal he
didn't have.

At the same moment, Rex saw
what she wanted to buy. It was a kind
of dinosaur she did not have in her
collection. She had never seen one
like it before.

Amanda saw what *she* wanted,
too. She ran for it. She reached for it.
And she felt two other hands on
hers.

Pinky and Rex and Amanda all
wanted the same thing.

"I *have* to have this dinosaur," Rex said. "I don't have one like it."

"But it's *pink*," said Pinky. "What do you want with a pink dinosaur? *I* have to have it, because it's pink and it's an animal I don't have already."

"You have *too* many animals, Pinky," said Amanda. "And Rex has too many dinosaurs. *I* should have it."

They made such a noise that Pinky's father came over with someone who worked in the store. "I'm afraid that is the last one we have," said the salesclerk.

"How much is it?" Pinky asked, digging into his pocket. He did not let go of the dinosaur.

"Three dollars and fifty cents," the salesclerk said.

Pinky's face fell. "I have *one* dollar and fifty cents," he said.

"Me, too," said Rex. She let go of the dinosaur. So did Pinky. Amanda looked surprised to find that she was holding it all by herself.

"I didn't want it, anyway," Rex said. "If I bought it, then I'd have twenty-eight dinosaurs and you'd have only twenty-seven animals."

"I know," said Pinky. "And if I bought it, I'd have twenty-eight animals and you'd have only twenty-seven dinosaurs. I didn't want it, either."

"Then *I* will buy it," said Amanda.

"Wait a minute!" Rex cried. "I have an idea, Pinky. Let's put our

money together and share it. You can keep it half the week, and I'll keep it the other half."

"And then we'll still have everything the same! Good thinking," said Pinky. They yanked the dinosaur out of Amanda's hands and ran to pay for it.

"What about *me*?" Amanda yelled.

Pinky and Rex put all their
money out on the counter.

"You have only three dollars,"
said the salesclerk. "You need fifty
cents more."

"I have fifty cents," they heard
someone say.

Pinky and Rex turned around.
Amanda had two quarters in her
hand and a big smile on her face.

"Sold!" said the clerk.

And so on Mondays and
Tuesdays and Wednesdays, the pink
dinosaur lives in Rex's room with all
her other dinosaurs. And on
Thursdays and Fridays and Saturdays,
the pink dinosaur lives in Pinky's
room with all his other animals.

And each and every Sunday, the pink dinosaur lives in Amanda's room—with Amanda.